The Song of Roland Smith

Jenny Koralek

The Song of Roland Smith

Illustrated by Peter Rush

PATRICK HARDY BOOKS

PATRICK HARDY BOOKS
28 Percy Street, London,
WIP 9FF, UK.

First published in Great Britain 1983
by Patrick Hardy Books

ISBN 0 7444 0015 5

Photoset by Rowland Phototypesetting Ltd
Bury St Edmunds, Suffolk
Printed and bound in Great Britain
at The Pitman Press, Bath

CONTENTS

To Benjamin

SIXES AND SEVENS

A self-portrait in poetry or prose.

That was our beastly homework.

I didn't mind the poetry or prose bit. Writing is my best thing.

But a self-portrait, a picture of myself?

Where did I begin? Face? And if face, which bit? Eyes? Nose? Did I have to say I bite my nails? What about how I felt? Did I *look* how I felt? How did I feel, anyway? Was I my face or my mood? Or *what?*

"A self-portrait," I said out loud alone in my room. "Trust Mr. Green to set something like that." He wasn't like the other teachers. He never wanted to know what we'd done in the holidays. I suppose that was too much to expect from someone who had taught Eskimos, worked in an umbrella factory and slept in the underground in World War Two.

7

I stood and stared at myself in the mirror.

I was even shorter and more freckled than I thought. I didn't often look in the mirror.

On that day, at that moment, I felt miserable.

"Oh well," I sighed. "Is it surprising since I'm so small for my age and a bit chubby and have such a stupid name? I suppose I could just tell the truth about myself as seen by me."

I sat down and was about to start writing when, through the slightly open door, I heard my mother talking to Great-Aunt Lundy who lives in our house.

"I don't know what's the matter with Roland. Ever since his last birthday he's been at sixes and sevens. He neglects his chores unless I shout and wherever he goes he dawdles. I really wonder about going off and leaving you to cope . . ."

My heart lurched. It was only two days till my mother went away to join my father. They wouldn't be back for a whole month.

"And he's not doing at all well at school," went on my mother. "Perhaps I should have a word with his teacher."

"You mean the one who always says such nice things about him in his reports, the one who likes his poems?" asked Aunt Lundy.

"Yes. That's Mr. Green. Poems are all very well, Aunt Lundy, a nice little hobby like pottery or playing duets, but poems don't pay the rent. No, Roland is a dissatisfied dreamer at present. I do hope it's just a passing phase." She sighed.

"Well, why don't you talk to Mr. Green," said Aunt Lundy, "if it'll put your mind at rest? You want to enjoy the Himalayas, after all."

I felt cross; so Aunt Lundy saw my reports, did she? I hate the way grown-ups are always showing people things, telling people things without asking first.

I felt sad too; I didn't want my mother to be unhappy.

When I was little I had a book in which each page was cut into three strips. I was surprised to see a book cut up like that, since I had been smacked once for trimming other books with my mother's sewing scissors. But this book was meant to be cut in pieces.

On page one was a giraffe, cut up into a head, a body and legs.

On page two there was a cut-up elephant.

On every page was a cut-up animal or bird. But if you muddled up the strips you got the funniest mixtures. Elephant's head with ostrich body and giraffe legs. Pig's snout with tiger stripes and a monkey's tail.

I don't know what sixes and sevens means really, but when my mother said it I thought of that book and knew that my head, body and legs did not seem to fit together at all well.

Anyway, if I was "all at sixes and sevens" it was my father's fault, first for being called Smith and second for getting my name wrong.

It was supposed to be Ronald.

I know that doesn't seem much better than

Roland, but it is. It's ordinary. I could have been Ron; that's like being Dave or Tom or Ted. It's the sort of name which helps you to join in.

But Roland is soft, and somehow you get looked at and then left out.

I know my father got it wrong out of kindness. He was so pleased to have a son that he went off up the street to tell all his friends. Of course they all wanted to drink a toast to me, so by the time he got to the place where you have to tell the baby's name, and they write it down on a form which you have to keep forever more, he got it wrong.

But the third reason why I blamed my father was because he'd gone to Mount Everest. He'd gone to take pictures of an expedition.

I missed him.

I'd tried boasting about him to the other boys at school, but since I had no proof that he'd gone to Mount Everest, no thrilling photographs or stamps, no smelly tuft of yak's hair, he might just as well have gone to Manchester or even to jail. They just didn't want to know.

I heard more talk through the open door.

"Perhaps he's tired," Aunt Lundy was saying. "Just as well it's half-term next week."

"Oh, Aunt Lundy," sighed my poor mother. "I wish he had a friend."

"You can't force these things," said Aunt Lundy, "but yes, he needs something to love – someone or something to look after."

"You mean a pet?"

"Why not?"

"I don't think a dog, somehow," replied my mother quickly.

A dog! I said to myself. Oh yes! Let it be a dog! A leaping, faithful hound. A companion by day, a guardian by night – for of course he'd sleep at the foot of my bed and I'd call him – call him what? Definitely not Rover. Why not Skipper? Nice and lively. No! Hannibal! That's it, Hannibal!

"No," said Aunt Lundy, "I wasn't thinking of a dog either."

My hopes were dashed, but I should have known better. My family are not dog-lovers. Anyway, I knew Aunt Lundy had other reasons for not wanting a dog.

They'll forget, I sighed, or fob me off with some dozy rodent.

"Why not a guinea pig or a hamster?" suggested Aunt Lundy. "They don't smell or take up too much room."

"Yes," said my mother. "We could manage that, I think."

I crept back to my homework. A guinea pig or a hamster, I groaned. How wet. How *tame*. I felt like howling, like baying to the moon – and at that very moment my song came to me. I sat down to write and it flowed onto the page like treacle off a spoon. Little did I know then how it would change my life.

Here it is:

THE SONG OF ROLAND SMITH

I am twelve years old
Size seven are my shoes
But I am not growing upwards
School is boring
And I hate my name
Aunt Lundy says hate is a strong word
But Roland leads to Roly
Roly leads to Poly
Roly-poly leads to gammon and spinach
And heigh-ho for some frog who would a wooing-go
I don't know what gammon is but I never eat spinach
Smith is plain and dull
Tiger in front of it would help
Or Roland the Rizzler
Names are important
They must fit just right
But Smith is plain and dull
Anyway there are too many Smiths
I counted 7,200 in the phone book
I'm tired of being ordinary
It's too little
I'd be scared to be extra-ordinary
It's too much
I'd like to be ordinary PLUS or even just plus
Take it or leave it but
This is my song.

II

A TALE OF THE UNEXPECTED

The next day things seemed much better.

I had my first long exciting letter from Dad.

I handed in my song, my homework, on time for once that term.

"Hope your self-portrait is a good blend of honesty *and* imagination, Roly," said Mr. Green. "Too much of one or the other makes very boring reading. Is it poetry or prose?"

"I don't know, Sir. It doesn't rhyme at the ends of the lines . . ."

"Ah, blank verse."

Blank verse? How could words be blank? I didn't like to ask.

"I don't know, Sir," I said again. "It – it sort of moans along – with a sound of its own."

"Hm," said Mr. Green. "A dirge. You're a bit young for dirges, aren't you?"

The bell rang and he hurried away before I could say *What's blank verse? What's a dirge?* All the same I liked the feeling of his interest. It was a friendly start to a new day.

But the best bit, the new bit, began in Geography.

The teacher made me stand up in front of the class and read some of my dad's letter out, because we were doing a project on *Man Against the Elements*.

It was very quiet in the classroom while I was reading from the letter about Sherpas, base camps, equipment and altitude sickness and the beauty of the foothills of the Himalayas. I had never thought

of flowers growing at the bottom of such high mountains.

All the boys believed me at last. They were really listening and specially Judd, who was sitting right in front that day because the teacher was tired of him sitting at the back not listening to anything.

When I came to Dad's last sentence: *I haven't seen a yeti yet,* they all laughed. Except Judd. He sat up straight and stared at me eagerly. I had always half-admired Judd, but I was also a bit scared of him. He was taller than me. Just by the way he walked you could tell he was on top of life. He was the same age as me, yet he had a Saturday job when my mother said I was still too young. His parents ran the best pet shop for miles around.

There was always a small crowd round him in the playground, laughing at his jokes or enjoying pieces of the large orange or two he "picked up" in the market on his way to school.

In the classroom Judd had the knack all right: he made you join in his own mischief, or he made you look guilty when it was really him all the time.

He made you pass notes or sherbet fountains along the row, and if you tried not to get involved he would look at you so sadly you felt you had spoiled the fun. Or "things" would happen to him which turned out to be all your fault, like the time he couldn't find his maths book and the teacher got really cross. When I stood up at the end of the lesson I'd been sitting on it all the time.

"Here it is, Sir!" cried Judd, who must have put it there himself. "Sorry, Sir. Fancy Roly not noticing." Then he smiled and winked as if we were both in a great plot against Them.

He also read books under the desk – he loved animal stories. Once I was caught out when Judd heard the teacher coming and shoved his book onto my lap. Of course I looked down – and I was the one who had to put all the chairs up after school that day.

It was mean of him not to own up and feeble, typically Rolyish, of me not to speak up. But I think Judd was sorry. He lent me a book about otters and never played tricks on me again.

So I had mixed feelings about Judd, but that day I felt proud when I saw how interested he was in what I was reading from Dad's letter. Proud then stunned.

When the bell rang Judd came straight up to me and clapped me on the shoulder.

"You're so *lucky*!" he cried. "You really are lucky, Roly! Think of having a dad like yours, out there, where you might see a yeti any minute. Gosh, I envy you. I wish I could see even the *footprint* of a yeti. I'm sick and tired of rabbits and guinea-pigs and budgies and even sicker of my big brother's ferrets. . . ."

"Ferrets?" I gulped.

"Yes, Ferrets," said Judd. "He keeps them in our backyard. Mum and Dad aren't keen to have them in the shop. But he does quite a trade on the side, as well as his hunting, as he calls it.

"Hunting?"

"Poaching more like," said Judd in a jealous voice. "Goes out at night. 'Course I'm never allowed to go with him."

"Well, at least you've got a Saturday job, which is more than I have,"

"Huh! It's only helping Mum and Dad to open up the shop. If I had a *yeti*," he dreamed aloud, "it would make Mike and his ferrets look very boring. People would come for miles to see me and my yeti."

Poor Judd! He seemed to feel more like me than I could ever have imagined. What was that funny old saying of Aunt Lundy's about other people's grass always looking greener than your own?

"Where would you keep a yeti – if you had one, that is?" I asked.

"Not *here*," said Judd. "I'd run away with it and live on a mountain top. No more ferrets, no more pet shop. No more school. Just me and my yeti! *You* could come and see us though."

"*Judd!*" I said. "Dad was only joking. Nobody knows if there really *is* a yeti. It's what's called a mythical beast."

"Huh!" cried Judd. "That just means nobody knows for sure, but they don't half hope it's real. Gosh, don't they half hope it's real. Well, I do. And it might exist. It just *might*. Listen, why don't you come back to my place for tea?"

I could hardly believe my ears. So many new things had happened in the last hour of an ordinary old school day. And now Judd himself was telling me his secret feeling and asking me home for tea! I had Dad to thank for this.

"Thanks a lot, Judd. I'd like to very much."

"Well, come on then. What are we waiting for?"

We dashed out into the street, whooping like cowboys to hide that funny mixture of shyness and happiness you sometimes feel.

Suddenly I thought of my song. How different it would have been if to-day had been yesterday. Some new lines blew into the tiny spaces between the whoops.

A friend, a friend.
Roland Smith has made a friend
Perhaps my song's not ready to end?

III

JUDD'S PLACE

Warmth, noise and delicious smells hit me as soon as Judd opened the front door of his house in Canal Street.

Then I got a shock.

"Is that you, George?" a bodiless voice shouted. "Well, come in then and shut the door. You're letting all the heat out!"

George? I said to myself. Had someone followed us in?

I half turned to look. Then it dawned on me. George was Judd! Or rather Judd was George. I stared at him and he gave me what was a sheepish look for the Judd I knew at school, and a wink.

So he had a name he didn't like either.

"I've brought a friend home for tea, Mum," Judd shouted through the noise of a radio and sounds of sizzling and washing up. In came Judd's mother with a big pot of tea.

"Hullo, boys," she said. "Only just got in myself and Grandad's creating for his tea. Your brother's gone out already because there's a new ferret he's after over Ridley way, and your dad'll be in any minute."

She drew breath, banged the tea-pot down on the table and fetched cups from the sideboard. A canary in the corner began to sing.

I could smell chips and sausages.

"Well then?" said Judd's mum. "Aren't you going to introduce me to your friend?"

"Yes, Mum. Sorry, Mum. This is Roly."

"Roly?" said Judd's mum with what I thought was a hidden giggle in her voice.

"Roland Smith," I said. "We're in the same class."

"That's nice," she shouted over the sizzling. "I like my boys to bring their friends home. George! Go and ask Grandad to turn that radio down – and while you're at it, take him his tea."

Judd obeyed and disappeared.

The radio suddenly stopped and the canary fell silent.

I stood in the middle of the room feeling shy but excited. It was so different here from my house.

Imagine having a brother who kept ferrets! And having chips and sausages straight after school.

Judd came back just as the front door banged open and shut behind a huge man.

"Hullo, son," said Mr. Tyler. "Who's this then?" he asked as he tossed down his coat and the evening paper.

"This is my friend, Roly," said Judd.

"Is that you, Harry?" shouted Judd's mother across our nods and hullos. "Tea's nearly ready, but our Mike's gone out."

"I know. I met him in the street. Says he's going over Ridley way . . ."

". . . after a new ferret," chimed in Judd and his mother as she came in carrying a tray loaded with food. Everybody laughed, and the canary began to sing again. It was all so jolly and friendly and noisy.

"Tuck in, boys!" said Judd's mum. "I thought we'd take ours in and keep Grandad company. He gets lonely with us out all day."

"Good idea!" said Mr. Tyler. "I'll come and give you a hand."

We munched our food for a while in comfortable silence. I felt we had known each other for years. I felt trusted and trusting enough to lean over and whisper, "I didn't know your real name was George."

"Hate it," mumbled Judd with his mouth full. "It sounds so dull and undaring. Stodgy. Georgy-porgy, pudding and pie – that's what they used to sing in the playground at my last school."

"And I get called Roly-poly pudding or gammon and spinach," I said. "What *is* gammon?"

"Posh ham," said Judd.

"Oh," I groaned. "I really do hate my name."

Judd grunted sympathetically. "It is a bit wet. Well, the name's wet, but you're not," he added kindly.

We drank our tea and ate our cake in a new and even warmer silence, the silence of true companions.

"Can I see the ferrets?" I asked.

"Yes," said Judd dolefully. "Everybody always wants to see the ferrets."

He led me out to the backyard, where there were several cages like rabbit-hutches. I peered into the gloom and could just make out some long, slinky, weaselly creatures.

"Ugh!" I stepped back quickly. "What's the big deal? They don't look much, and they don't half stink!"

"You're right. But they're *savage*," Judd whispered, with awe. "You should see them go after a rabbit. They've got fangs and they look horrible with blood dripping down their teeth."

"Ugh! I'd rather have a hound, or a kestrel on my wrist, than an outsize stoat for a pet."

"Would you?" asked Judd. "Would you really?"

"George! Roland!" called Judd's mother from the bright doorway. "George, it's time to wash up, and you, Roland, it's getting dark now. Shouldn't you be off home?"

I looked at the luminous digital watch Dad had given me when he went away.

"Seven o'clock!" I yelped. "Thanks for the tea, Mrs. Tyler!"

"Any time, Roland," she said.

"Meet me at the shop tomorrow at ten o'clock," hissed Judd. "I'll have something for you."

Although I ran all the way home and arrived virtuously out of breath, I couldn't escape my mother's wrath.

"Where on earth have you been?" she pounced as soon as I came in.

"Over to Judd's for tea," I muttered.

"Judd who? And *who* is Judd?" put in Aunt Lundy, leaning over the banister.

"He's a boy in my class."

"Well, I do think you might have let us know. Another time, ask if you can 'phone!" snapped my mother.

"Yes, Roly, your mother was worried. Try to be more thoughtful."

"Sorry," I mumbled.

"Go to your room," said my mother coldly. "No supper, no telly."

"And goodnight!" said Aunt Lundy.

I obeyed. I was sorry – but I was also very glad that tea at Judd's house was more than a cup of PG Tips and ginger biscuits for dunking that we have at my house after school.

IV

SURPRISES

"Eat your bacon sandwich, smartish," said my mother at breakfast-time. "My taxi's coming at ten and I'd like you to bring my bags down."

How could I have forgotten? It was Saturday! She was leaving on her long journey to join my father. What would it be like to be without them both for the first time in my life? What would it be like, alone with Aunt Lundy?

"Are you excited?" I asked my mother. I tried to sound bright and unselfish.

"Yes, I am. It's always been my dream to see those mountains."

Her eyes smiled into mine and told me she saw what I was trying to hide.

"I'll send you a post-card every day," she said. "Now eat up. Aunt Lundy is going to start calling you any minute, I have a feeling in my bones."

"Why?" I asked.

"Wait and see," said my mother. "I was right to be cross with you last night," she added.

"Mm, I know."

"But I was crosser than I might have been, because Aunt Lundy had been waiting for you to come in from school since four o'clock."

"Why? Whatever for?"

"Surprise!" said Aunt Lundy peering round the doorway and pushing at her wispy hair. "Come into the hall and see what I got for you *yesterday*, you wretched boy!"

I followed Aunt Lundy and my mother followed me. On the floor was an old, silent shoe-box. I moved towards it.

"Wait!" cried Aunt Lundy. "Does he deserve it, I ask myself?"

"Does he indeed?" agreed my mother.

I thought they winked at each other, but as the light is bad in our hall I could not be sure.

"Will he care for it?" tantalised Aunt Lundy.

"Care for what?" I asked.

"Open it and see!" cried Aunt Lundy.

I approached the box and opened it. Nestling in a corner, fast asleep, was . . . . a hamster.

I remembered the conversation I had overheard. I remembered they worried about me. I remembered also talk of yetis and ferrets, kestrels and hounds. I remembered my song.

But what could I do, except give Aunt Lundy and my mother hugs and show signs of surprise and joy?

I sat down and tenderly stroked the top of the sleeping hamster's head.

"Thank you, Aunt Lundy." I said. "I think I'll call him Everest."

"Everest?" said my mother.

"Funny name for a hamster," said Aunt Lundy.

They didn't get the joke. What better name for a little furry sleeping ball?

Luckily another good reason for it flashed into my mind.

"In memory of Dad," I said brightly.

"I think you mean as a reminder of Dad," smiled my mother.

I nodded and smiled back.

"He'll need a little cage with a wheel," my mother was saying. "Here, Roly, this is my contribution." And she handed me five pounds.

"That's great, Mum. Thanks very much."

"Why don't you go up to the pet shop as soon as your mother's on her way?" said Aunt Lundy. "Poor little creature's been cooped up long enough in that old shoe-box."

What a stroke of luck: a good reason for going out tossed into my lap. I hadn't really wanted to tell them I was going to meet Judd. Not after last night.

Then suddenly, I felt badly about everything. I hadn't thought to 'phone. I didn't do my chores. I did dawdle. Yet they'd bought me a pet, and now my mother was leaving.

"Well," I said, "I'll just bring your luggage down, Mum."

"Thank you, Roly."

My feet took me lightly enough up the stairs, but I felt heavy.

I wanted to say a real "thank you" and a real "sorry", but at that moment the door-bell rang.

It was the taxi.

As I came down again my mother was pulling on her coat and Aunt Lundy was opening the door. My mother hugged me hard.

"I know you hate saying good-bye," she said softly.

"It's short for 'God be with you'," said Aunt Lundy from the doorway. My mother flashed Aunt Lundy a signal which said: *Don't say things like that. You know it annoys.*

To my surprise it didn't annoy me. It didn't annoy me at all.

"Could you wash up the breakfast things and empty the bins for Aunt Lundy before you go up to the pet shop?" asked my mother, snapping her bag shut.

"Sure," I said.

I hugged her then and fixed a kiss near her ear.

"Good-bye, Mum. Give my love to Dad."

I ran into the kitchen and poured a lot of washing-up liquid into the sink and turned the taps full on. It was good to have something to do. I whizzed through the washing-up, emptied the bins and pocketed the five-pound note.

I found I was whistling.

Free at last! Judd's voice had been tight and

excited last night. I had a feeling he had an adventure up his sleeve. If so, I wanted to be there and in it.

I opened the front door.

"Roly!" called Aunt Lundy from the top of the stairs. "Roly, be a dear. Bring me a pomegranate from the market!"

She has this passion for exotic fruits.

"Sure," I cried, hastily shutting the door behind me before she asked for a mango or a paw-paw. I decided to go to the market on my way and to buy the pomegranate before I forgot. Didn't want to be in Aunt Lundy's bad books on our very first day alone together.

It was when I had paid for the pomegranate and was standing at the fruit stall in the noise and bustle,

dazzled by colours and smells, that I had a tempting thought: *If Judd could pinch an orange once in a while, why not me?*

How should I go about it?

I dawdled past a few stalls, feeling slightly sick. How did you get your hand round an apple or a handful of cherries without being spotted at once? As for getting them *hidden* – the gap between the stall and my pocket seemed wider than a ravine in the Grand Canyon.

Suddenly I knew: I just couldn't do it.

I wanted so much to be more like Judd – cool and daring. But it was no good. I was me, Roland Smith. It seemed I couldn't go against myself. If I wanted Judd to think I was great it would have to be in some way which was my very own.

I shuffled my feet in some fallen cabbage leaves and made my way to the Tyler's pet shop. I marched in and found myself face to face with Judd's Dad.

V

A RISKY OUTING

"Hello, lad! New customer, eh? Or are you looking for George?" smiled Mr. Tyler.

George? Who was George? I had to think. Poor Judd. George is a very splodgy name.

"Both. Someone's given me a hamster and I need a cage with a wheel, some sawdust and, er – well, some hamster food, please."

"Right you are!" boomed Judd's dad. He reached into the window for a smart blue cage with a neat little wheel. "One cage, one bag sawdust and one bag grain coming up." He banged the items onto the counter and I handed over my fiver.

Mr. Tyler pinged the cash register.

"Won't see much change out of this," he said. "Still, can't have something for nothing. Want to go through and see George? He's out the back – nearly time for him to knock off."

"Thanks. I thought he might like to come and help me get Everest settled."

"*Everest?*" echoed Judd's dad.

"My hamster," I said politely.

"Everest?" he said again. "Funny name for a hamster."

"Yes, but it's in memory of my dad. Oh, no," I remembered, "I mean, it's a reminder of my dad."

"I *see*," laughed Mr. Tyler. He lifted up the counter to let me into the back. "Mind how you go. And watch out for Parker in there. He's a noisy bird – belonged to a sergeant major."

I shoved the bags into the cage and staggered off.

It was quite dark in the room at the back of the shop.

"Judd?" I called.

"Bettah late than nevah!" screeched a bossy voice in my ear. I jumped a few feet but at least I didn't die of shock.

"Shut up Parker," said another voice.

"Judd?" I called. "Is that you? Where are you?"

"Ssh! Over here!" The urgent voice of my friend came at me through the dark.

"Come and see what I've got and then let's beat it quick."

"Can't see a thing. You sound like something on the telly."

Judd came into the light of the door that opened onto the street. He was wearing an anorak which bulged, as if he'd been stuffing himself with chips and jam butties ever since I last saw him. But the anorak not only bulged. It wriggled and snuffled. Before my very eyes a little wet nose peeped out, followed by dark brown eyes and crumpled ears.

I dropped onto my knees and tried to stroke him.

This was Hannibal!

"Oh Judd!" I cried. "Can we play with him? He's the little dog of my dreams! Where were you taking him anyway?"

"I told you I'd have something for you, didn't I?" whispered Judd, pushing the puppy back down inside his anorak. "Of *course* you can play with him, but not here. Come on! Follow me!"

Eagerly I scrambled to my feet. Oh yes, I heard the *buts* – *but* we shouldn't without asking – *but* it's a kind of stealing.

BUT, said the loudest *but*, *BUT* you've been longing for just this: a dog, a friend . . .

"Don't muck about," advised Parker. "Don't muck about."

Judd was already out of the door.

"Coming!" I whispered. "Wait for me!"

Down the street we scarpered, heading for the park on the hill with the three ponds at the bottom of it. By the time we got there my arms were stiff from clutching the cage with its noisy whizzing wheel. I put it down and flung myself onto the grass.

Hannibal struggled out of Judd's jacket. He jumped straight at me, licking my face all over. His deep dark eyes were trusting; his pointed ears alert to life. His nose was damp and cool and his tongue showed pink as he panted and grinned. His tail wagged and thumped. He was wonderful: an Alsatian pup ready to romp all day and stand guard all night. A very long piece of string trailed down from his little collar. I grabbed the string and turned to Judd with a smile.

"What's this cage, then?" asked Judd.

"It's for Everest,"

"Everest?" chortled Judd.

How he laughed when I told him the whole sorry tale. He saw the sad joke in the name; of course he did. He was my friend.

Then we got down to the fun.

The sun was shining; wild-shaped clouds scudded across blue sky and kite-flyers were gathering on the hilltop for a competition, but all our interest for now was on Hannibal. He bounded about, tugging on the string.

We charged down the hill with the puppy tearing at our heels. In and out at the edges of the three ponds we splashed. The puppy shook himself and drenched us. We went wild then, all three of us, wild in the wind. We threw sticks for him which he quickly learned to bring back, and for a while we let go his string. He ran off into the bushes, so we chased and scrambled after him, grabbed hold of the string, ran up the hill again and all collapsed in a panting heap. I wound the string loosely round my wrist and Hannibal fell asleep.

It was great lying there looking up at the sky and the pillowy clouds.

Judd fidgeted a little, dipped his hand into his pocket and produced a large orange. He peeled it and passed half to me.

"Fell off the back of a lorry, did it?" I teased.

"Cheeky, aren't we?" said Judd.

He grinned at me.

"Do you often do it?" I asked.

"Not really. I never take anything else. It's the colour, see. It's so bright. Sort of catches your eye. . ."

"I tried to . . . this morning."

"Tried what?" said Judd, licking orange juice off his fingers.

"To . . .er. . . steal one. Couldn't do it."

"Doesn't go with you, Roly," said Judd. "Nicking fruit, or anything else, come to that. It's not such a big deal anyway. I'm thinking of packing it in. I've sort of gone off oranges."

"You could say we were both thieves now."

"What do you mean? Oh, the pup? Don't be daft, Roly. We've only borrowed him for a bit."

Hannibal was stirring. I patted him tenderly and lay back on the grass. I felt happy, lucky, excited.

Just then a great shout came from the kite-flyers. We looked up to see dragons, boxes and huge, bright butterflies disappearing into the far sky.

"Imagine the feel of it!" cried Judd. "To know how to let out a string and then how to pull on a string so that you can get a flimsy thing to fly almost out of sight."

I stared at the soaring kites and imagined. So strong was my imagining that the tugging of Hannibal on the string turned into me flying a kite and soon I was lost away up there in that far, far sky.

Until Judd brought me down to earth with a loud yell.

"Roly! Roly! He's gone. Hannibal has gone!"

VI

HULLABALOO

At first we ran about in crazy blind circles and zigzags, yelling our heads off.

"Hannibal! Hannibal!" we called. He did not come.

We stood side by side and tried to call him in firm, calm voices.

Still he did not come.

East, west, north and south we went, carefully searching, calling all the time. But Hannibal did not come panting and bounding, leaping and licking, back to us. He had gone – back to the ponds? Drowned? Out of the park onto the busy road? Run over? Stolen? Had we been watched?

We looked at each other and trembled.

"It's no good, Roly," groaned Judd. "He's vanished."

"What'll we do?" I cried.

"We must go home and tell Mum and Dad and the p-p-police," stammered Judd.

My heart turned over and my palms began to sweat. I shut my eyes.

"It's a nightmare."

"No, it's not," said Judd. "It's real. The most really horrible thing that's ever happened to me." His voice shook.

I looked at my watch. It was long past lunch-time.

"What time does the shop shut?"

"Five-thirty on Saturdays," said Judd. "It's our busiest day."

"If they haven't already noticed he's missing, they're bound to when they shut up shop."

"'Course," said Judd. "Heck and hell, we're for it now. My dad'll kill us."

I could just imagine Mr. Tyler in a rage.

"We-ell," I said, with knocking knees and trembling tongue. "I don't think they'll like it much if we come in now, when they're busy, and suddenly tell them we've lost a valuable pup."

"And he had a pedigree," sighed Judd.

"A pedigree?" I squeaked. "Oh no! We really are in trouble."

"But at least he's got his collar on," said Judd more brightly. "With the shop's address on it. Someone may find him and bring him back. There are some decent people, you know."

"Yes, of course there are," I agreed, but secretly I

knew that if I found a beautiful pup like Hannibal running loose I'd be torn in half between the wrong of keeping him and the right of taking him home to his owner.

I looked at Judd and saw him reading my thoughts just as if they were in a balloon over my head.

"But Judd," I said, "it would be very difficult for a kid to come marching home with a stray pup. His family would want to know where on earth he got it from."

"Sure," said Judd, "but a real dog-thief, he'd have a hiding place and – "

"Look," I interrupted, "it's no good us standing here just *yattering*. We've got to go and tell someone quickly. Let's run back to my place and get Aunt Lundy to phone your mum and dad so's they can report it to the police."

"Good idea, Roly," cried Judd, and I could hear relief in his voice.

It crossed my mind then that it might not be that easy to get Aunt Lundy to do our dirty work for us, but I could see that Judd was as scared as I was of going straight to his father. I did not really believe he'd actually *kill* us, but might not a man who boomed and blew with jolliness also boom and blow into a dreadful fury?

"Don't forget your cage," Judd was saying. "You've still got Everest to think of."

I picked up the awkward cage, its silly little empty wheel going round and round, and we set off as fast as we could, both knowing that whichever way we came at it, we were about to face a terrible storm.

The nearer we got to home, the slower our footsteps became.

Suddenly Judd came to a halt.

"It's no good, Roly," he said shakily. "We can't put all that on your aunt. We must do it ourselves–at once. If you go straight to the police and I go to the shop it'll s-save time."

I looked at his pale face. He was braver than I was. It was true, we couldn't for long run away from the consequences of what we'd done.

"If you're brave enough to go and tell your mum and dad, well, I've just got to be brave enough to go to the police," I said.

"Well – go on then," said Judd. "Get a move on."

Then he was running at the speed of light – never even waved. Now it began to sink in. This was real: out of dreams and words we'd made something happen. A real dog, a real outing, real fun. Out of dreams and words, too, we'd lost Hannibal. Judd was right – I must get a move on, do something.

I charged off towards the police station. How do they set about finding lost dogs? Would I get a ride in a patrol car? Would they use the siren?

As I panted into the police station a blustering human cannonball shot out of the door, straight into me. I leapt back from the impact, and found myself face to face with Mr. Tyler.

He took one look at me, grabbed hold of me and

sank his fingers into my arm, really hard. His anger nearly blew me sky high.

"What are *you* doing here?" he shouted. "Where's George? You thieving, thoughtless little good-for-nothings!"

"G-George's gone to look for you at the shop," I stammered. "We decided it'd be quicker if George went home to tell you and I came straight to the police. We've lost him, Mr. Tyler," I blubbered. "We've lost your dog."

Mr. Tyler let go my arm and stood back. He was silent for ages, all his bluster gone.

"*Lost* him?" he said very, very quietly. "Lost him, you said? Why he's dead, boy, dead. Run over and reported not half an hour ago. And all because of a silly, careless caper. D'you think I couldn't see at once it was an inside job? Why, I could shake you till your teeth rattled." His voice began to rise again.

"Just wait till I get my hands on George. It'd make me feel better to beat the living daylights out of the both of you but that won't bring back my pedigree dog."

Mr. Tyler was trembling from head to foot and I burst into tears.

A great shadow fell across us both for a moment. Mr. Tyler became quiet again. For the first time I discovered that sometimes it doesn't make any difference at all how sorry you are for what you've done. There was nothing to say, or do. I felt sick.

"Here, blow your nose," said Mr. Tyler gruffly, passing me his handkerchief. "What's done's done, and I'll not lay a hand to you. But you won't forget today in a hurry and, if I have anything to do with it, nor will George."

He started to move away, homewards.

"I'll tell you one thing, though. I'm not having you and George together again. You keep away from each other. What's wrong with you youngsters nowadays? Anything goes! In my day you'd have felt the back of somebody's hand and gone without your dinners for a fortnight."

I stood there bent and bowed and only when he disappeared from sight did I creep home to Aunt Lundy.

She was waiting for me at the door.

Silently I held out the pomegranate. Silently she took it.

"What did you call the dog?" she asked.

"Hannibal," I said in a watery voice. "But how – ?"

Aunt Lundy raised her hand.

"It's all right. I know all about it. The Tylers have been on the 'phone, on and off, for ages. I thought we'd have high tea and then go and see those Laurel and Hardy shorts at the Electric."

I opened and shut my mouth a few times.

"No," she said, "not one word tonight. I've told the Tylers, and I'm telling you. We're all to sleep on it. Besides, tomorrow's Sunday."

VII

BLUE SUNDAY

I woke next day to the smell of Sunday dinner. For a minute I was dazed. It wasn't like me to sleep in so long. Then I remembered yesterday.

Suddenly I felt as if twenty butterflies were fighting to get out of my stomach.

I jumped out of bed and rushed downstairs.

Aunt Lundy was in the kitchen humming to herself and whisking away at something frothy in a pudding bowl.

"Good morning, young man," she called. "Or should I say 'good afternoon'? Had a good sleep?"

"Er, yes, thankyou, but, Aunt Lundy, what are we going to do?"

"Do?" said Aunt Lundy. "Why, when this Yorkshire pudding's ready we're going to sit down like two civilised human beings and have our Sunday lunch. That's what we're going to do. Business as usual, that's my motto."

I watched her pour batter into the baking tray.

45

Gosh, she was cool and calm. She didn't spill a drop.

"Open the oven door please, Roly. Now hurry up and get dressed. You've got five minutes. The oven's very hot."

From the door I tried again.

"But what about . . . ?" I began.

"What about what?" interrupted Aunt Lundy. "Oh *that*. Get dressed. Fetch the cider and we'll talk about *that* over lunch. Hurry *up* or it'll all spoil!"

I shot upstairs, pulled on my jeans, grabbed a clean shirt, passed a damp flannel across my face and raced down to the larder for the cider. I arrived back in the kitchen just as Aunt Lundy was carving the joint.

"You forgot to brush your hair," said Aunt Lundy, putting a steaming plate in front of me. "Well, aren't you going to pour?"

Hastily I filled two glasses with cider and waited for her to sit down.

"Tuck in," said Aunt Lundy. We passed the mustard to each other. I was ravenous and for a few minutes we ate in enjoyable silence.

"Very good sermon this morning," said Aunt Lundy. "And *two* of my favourite hymns."

"Aunt Lundy!" I cried. "Half the day's gone by with me asleep and you at church! What am I going to do about the Tylers, and Judd, and what happened yesterday?"

"I've also been to the pub," remarked Aunt Lundy.

"The pub?" I echoed. "You don't usually go to the pub, do you?"

"No!" laughed Aunt Lundy. "I met your Mr. Green on the way home from church. Second helpings?"

"No, no . . . What was Mr. Green doing round here? He lives right on the other side of town."

"He was on his way to see *you*, Roly. Nearly went next door. Got the number of the house wrong. Stopped to ask me if I knew the Smiths. I said yes. We got talking. I introduced myself. Repaired to the Eagle."

"Repaired to the Eagle?" I asked.

"Went to the pub then, if you like short words," grinned Aunt Lundy.

"Why was he coming to see me – and on a Sunday?" I racked my brains. I hadn't done anything wrong – not at school at any rate – not for ages.

"About your homework, Roly, your poem," said Aunt Lundy.

I jumped. I'd forgotten all about my self-portrait in poetry or prose.

"He showed it to me, Roly," Aunt Lundy went on. "I must say I had no idea how disgruntled you've been feeling."

"Disgruntled?" I repeated.

"Discontented. Unhappy. Fed up. No wonder you got carried away by an adventure with Judd. I don't suppose he's really such a bad lad."

"No, he's not," I said indignantly. "He only took

the dog for me because he knew how much I've always wanted one."

"Oh," said Aunt Lundy. "I see. Yes, really, I do see. A hamster's not exactly a boy's companion, is it? Oh dear!" She sighed. "Perhaps your mother and I are to blame for not letting you have a dog of your own." She sighed again.

"Clear the plates, Roly. Ice cream?"

"No, thanks, I'm full."

Suddenly I felt heavy inside.

"What's Mr. Green going to do? What did he say?" I asked.

"Oh, he's coming back for tea – with the Tylers," said Aunt Lundy, beginning to wash up.

"Wh-what for?" I stammered, groping for a tea towel.

"Why, to help, of course. I told him all about the dog – what did you say his name was?"

"Hannibal," I muttered.

"Naturally, Mr. Tyler's very angry. He wants you both severely punished. And Mr. Green is your form teacher. He knows you *and* Judd. You need allies, if we're to sort this thing out properly. Besides, I like your Mr. Green. Have you fed Everest?"

"No."

"Well, do so. I'm off for a quick doze. Keep your ears open for the doorbell around four."

And she disappeared to her room.

Everest was living up to his name; fast asleep in his nesting-box. He didn't stir when I noisily filled his

48

feeding-tray. I wondered if he'd ever discover the little wheel.

It was hours till four o'clock.

Perhaps I should write to Mum and Dad and tell them what had happened. How long would it take a letter to reach the Himalayas? I wondered. It would only worry them, and anyway I didn't know the end of the story yet.

I climbed the stairs slowly to my room and stared at myself in the mirror.

"Roland Smith," I said out loud. "Roland Smith, see what happens when you try to be what you're not? Disaster all round."

I decided to write a poem about Hannibal. I picked up my pen and fished my very private note-book from its hiding-place.

I sat and sat, but the words just would not come. I could find no rhymes to fit the story of Hannibal.

I couldn't write. I couldn't cry. I wasn't even afraid of what Mr. Tyler's punishment might be.

The sadness was silent, like stone.

Then the doorbell rang.

VIII

RAILWAY TEA AND RESCUE

"Aunt Lundy," I called.

There was no reply. Scared as anything, I called again.

"Aunt Lundy! They're here."

"I'll be down in a minute," she answered this time. "Go and let them in!"

I crept downstairs and opened the front door.

There stood a jumbly crowd: the Tylers with poor Judd in tow, and Mr. Green. They'd obviously met on the doorstep and the atmosphere was tense with unspoken questions. A sort of satisfaction was coming from Mr. Tyler at the sight of our teacher. It just showed how serious our crime was, Mr. Tyler all but said by his look.

I began to feel it was true. All these grown-ups gathered together at my house, all because of us. It was a truly awful sight.

"Come in," I said in a high voice, like a girl.

"Yes, come in, come in!" came Aunt Lundy's voice comfortingly close behind me. "Come on up to my room, all of you. You'll all be much more comfortable there." Aunt Lundy pushed at her wispy hair, straightened her specs and rubbed her hands together. She shone with sureness and strength.

"I'll lead the way," she beamed, tripping away up the stairs. "We'll have a good cup of tea and attend properly to the matter of these boys." Mr. and Mrs. Tyler obediently followed her, with Mr. Green bringing up the rear.

For a moment Judd and I were left standing in the hall. Judd started to speak, but I put a finger to my lips.

"Come up too, boys!" called Aunt Lundy from the landing. "I need you to make the tea."

I knew then that Aunt Lundy was definitely on our side. Once inside her room they'd all be spellbound and she'd have her way. So far in my life I've never seen another room like Aunt Lundy's. I had even forgotten how much I loved it until I stepped into it with my new friend that day. The past was in it, and suddenly it made the present much bigger because the future lay there too. I looked across at Judd. Did he feel it too? Did he feel lighter and brighter in this cluttered, cosy room?

The furniture was old: a huge armchair to curl up in, that is, if you got there before Ross and Cromarty who lay there now, intertwined and fast asleep: two huge six-toed tabby cats. There they were – the reason, in a vast ball of fur, why I had known I'd never get my dog.

Hundreds of books lined one wall; on another was Aunt Lundy's poster collection: cartoons first, from World War Two. The one I liked best asked: *Is your journey really necessary?* It was a question I often put to myself as I trudged to school. Next came Winston Churchill, various kings and queens, Superman and the Beatles. Aunt Lundy loved the Beatles.

"*All the lonely people,*" she would sing over the washing up.

"They're so *right*," she would say. "Where *do* they all come from?"

On the mantelpiece were dozens of photos in polished silver frames.

"Ancestors, ancestors," was all she would tell me about them. "I'm making a family tree for you, and when it's finished we'll match them up one rainy day when you have really absolutely nothing better to do."

But her pride and joy was her 'forties radio, or wireless, as she called it, on which all the stations of the world were printed: Warsaw, Hilversum, Stockholm . . . "None of those silly numbers," she would say with scorn. She still tuned in morning and night to the shipping forecasts. "We had to, in the War," was her excuse. "Old habits die hard, you know."

Exotic shells and corals lay on the window shelves and perched in one corner sat a chubby little stone man whom Aunt Lundy called "my laughing Buddha".

"Picked him up in the Far East," she once told me.

"Ah, Roly," she'd sighed happily, "I've had a long life, full of adventures. And now? I just love my room, my cats, people to tea and – and pomegranates!"

"Roly! Stop day-dreaming!" Aunt Lundy's voice cut sharply through my thoughts. "Railway tea, Roly! Show Judd the drill."

Railway tea was her answer to all troubles, from cold feet to end-of-holidays gloom. Strong tea, in large mugs, with milk and plenty of sugar.

Under cover of the noisy, boiling kettle and clanking of mugs Judd whispered, "I think your aunt's really great. Smashing room!"

Settled on sturdy old cushioned chairs at the old round table, the Tylers looked dazed. I think they were feeling shy. Mr. Green was peering around, nodding and smiling as if he already knew the room, and loved it.

"You always fill the mugs too full," said Aunt Lundy as we plonked the tea down on the table. "Judd, fetch the sugar."

Mr. Tyler jumped. "Judd?" he spluttered. "Hang on a bit! Who's Judd, I'd like to know?"

Judd blushed and stirred his tea very fast and for far too long. Mr. Green looked puzzled.

Aunt Lundy leant forward. "What's your real name, Judd?" she asked.

"George," muttered Judd.

"Call yourself Judd at school, eh?" she pursued. "To make you sound more interesting? I know – a *tough guy*?"

"Something like that," said Judd. "Got it out of a book."

"Well, well!" cried Mr. Tyler. "You never know the half of it."

"And only then if you're lucky," put in Mrs. Tyler, sadly. "Whatever possessed you boys?" she sniffed.

Bravely Judd spoke up.

"It's true, I took Hannibal – well, borrowed him, from the shop. We just took him up for a romp. We were going to bring him back, we really were, although I wished Roly could keep him forever, but he said he'd never be allowed to keep a dog – and . . . and . . ."

My heart ached. He'd had to leave so much out. You can hardly ever tell grown-ups all the bits in between.

Then Mr. Tyler fairly flew off the handle.

"What a pair! I've said it before and I'll say it again. The next thing, they'll be vandalizing cars and 'phone boxes. I don't want you two going out

together again. Looking for a bit of excitement, were you, eh? Get a bit bored now and then, eh? Wonder what else you get up to behind our backs? In my day you'd have had your backsides tanned."

"Yes, they would," agreed Aunt Lundy. "That's absolutely so."

Mr. Tyler was so amazed he shut up.

"And you, Mr. Green," Aunt Lundy went on, "do you agree with Mr. Tyler?"

"Looking for excitement often leads to trouble," said Mr. Green mildly, "but something good often comes out of something bad, I believe."

"As you, perhaps, know – better than some of us," said Aunt Lundy. Mr. Green nodded. Many secrets, it seemed, danced between them.

"Well," interrupted Mr. Tyler impatiently. "What's to be done? What's it all add up to, I ask?"

"I have a plan," said Aunt Lundy firmly. "Let's take a *wide* view. Mr. Green and I have already had a word, and we agree that separating the boys won't help one little bit. It'd be much better if they did something together that was" – she paused – "constructive and responsible." The long, strong words hung in the air, which had grown still. "And here's Mr. Green," she went on, "willing to take them on – just for a couple of days. They'd be down by the sea, out of doors, out of mischief, but above all, Mr. Green tells me, they'd be a very real help." Her eyes had a faraway look, as if she could see something unknown to us, and full of surprises.

"Are you sure you're right?" asked Mrs. Tyler, half-anxious, half-impressed.

"I'm sure I'm right," said Aunt Lundy positively.

"What'll it cost?" asked Mr. Tyler gruffly.

"Goodwill all round, and rubber boots," said Mr. Green, and turned to Judd and me. "We'd set off tomorrow after breakfast; meet you both outside the church and bring you back on Tuesday."

"All right, everyone?" asked Aunt Lundy. "Mr. Tyler, Mrs. Tyler? What do you think? Shall we give it a try?"

"We-ell," said Mrs. Tyler, "Mr. Green *should* know best. After all, he is their teacher."

Mr. Tyler stood up.

"All right," he said wearily. "Give it a go. But if it doesn't work, then we'll try *my* way."

"So good of you all to come," smiled my wonderful, magical old aunt. Chattering and murmuring, she ushered everyone downstairs and, with a final cluster of thankyous, closed the front door on them. She turned to me.

"I need another cup of tea, Roly!" she gasped. "And you'd better get ready for Mr. Green. He's a brick! It *is* a good idea, you'll see – and besides, you'll be company for Percy."

IX

MEETING PERCY

"Climb in," said Mr. Green on the dot of ten o'clock next morning. "Better both sit in the back, then I can't be accused of having favourites."

Already he'd quickly bundled our bags into the boot.

"Want to get back to Percy as quickly as possible."

Judd turned to me mouthing the words "Who's P . . .?" but Mr. Green went straight on. "Barney's only just arrived. He'll need time to settle, I suppose."

He set off at a mighty sharp speed, heading for the coast road. The sea is only about ten miles from our town.

Silently Judd pointed to a rough old sheath knife on his belt.

"Got it off my brother," he mouthed. "You can gut rabbits with it."

Silently I produced a compass from my pocket.

"Might come in handy," I mouthed back, although I doubted it very much. Mr. Green seemed to know exactly where he was going.

"You boys are very quiet," said Mr. Green.

"Where are we actually going, Sir?" asked Judd.

"I've got an old barn on the farm behind Gull's Cove," said Mr. Green. "We use it in the holidays and at week-ends. We've fixed it up a bit, so we can have people to stay."

Percy, Barney, we . . . . Mr. Green had been talking in riddles ever since we got into the car. I was beginning to feel that even if he and Aunt Lundy had saved us from separation, and perhaps a beating and starvation, we were certainly not going to be let off lightly. Something else was in store for us. Perhaps Mr. Green went round collecting real vandals and thieves and thought Judd and I could learn something from being with criminals. I'd seen a programme about something like that on television. In America, that was.

"Excuse me, Sir," I spoke up at last. "Who's *we*?"

"Just my wife, Percy and me," said Mr. Green, slowing down a bit. "I promised them I'd drive carefully," he added with a grin. "Well, and now there's Barney too."

Judd and I exchanged quite desperate looks.

Percy must be a positive weed, I was thinking. What a name! Even worse than mine.

"Anyhow, it'll be just the four of us, I'm afraid."

The four of us? I'd already counted six.

"Four?" said Judd, also doing his sums. "I make it six."

"Oh, no, 'fraid not," said Mr. Green. "I put my wife on the train while I was on my way to fetch you this morning. She's gone on a painting course, and Percy and I are going to join her for the last few days of half-term. Then we'll all come home together. So it's just the four of us, because Barney in that sense doesn't count."

Barney, in that sense, doesn't count.

Again Judd and I looked at each other.

"The weather's looking pretty good," said Mr. Green. "Let's hope we can get out for some walks. There's a lovely little church out on the headland I'd like you to see."

Judd nudged me. I nudged back, but we held our tongues. What fun we were going to have!

"Know how to chop wood?" asked Mr. Green.

"No-no, Sir!"

"Yes, Sir!" said Judd.

"We could have supper out," said Mr. Green. That sounded better. "Fresh mackerel and baked potatoes." Better still. "Know how to fish?"

"No-no, Sir!"

"Yes, Sir," said Judd.

"Row?" asked Mr. Green, changing gear as we came to the steep narrow road leading to Gull's Cove.

"Yes, Sir!" I cried.

"No, Sir," said Judd.

61

"Well, we'll teach you," said Mr. Green, pulling up outside a ramshackle barn with some huge sunflowers standing guard over its doorway. "Percy likes to take a turn with the oar."

Well, it was good to know that weedy Percy liked to do *something* energetic. And Barney? Did he row too, I wondered?

"Here we are," said Mr. Green. "Out you hop. You're in for a noisy welcome, I warn you!"

A noisy welcome? From Percy and Barney? He must be joking.

Judd and I grinned at each other and climbed out of the car.

The minute we did so there was merry pandemonium – first barking and then a bell-like voice, calling:

"Barney, Barney! Sit! It's *Dad's* car. Just coming, Dad! I'm on the last page of my book and it's so funny!"

"Come in boys," said Mr. Green.

We followed him through the door into a friendly, muddly room.

"Everything all right?" asked Mr. Green. "Is Barney doing his stuff?"

Percy was curled up in an armchair. Her fingertips ran speedily over the last page of her book, but her nice-looking freckly face was turned towards us. Her free hand rested on Barney's thick, raised collar.

Yes, Percy was a girl, a little older than Judd and me. Barney was a fully grown Alsatian with a shining coat of fur. The ghost of what Hannibal might have been, perhaps – a special dog.

"Don't fuss, Dad!" said Percy. "Everything's fine! And, gosh, you were quick. You must have been driving too fast as usual. Barney and I have been sitting here quietly, getting to know each other. Well, aren't you going to introduce me to the terrible two?"

She stood up.

"Which is Judd? Which is Roly?"

Judd and I just stood there, speechless.

Barney was a dog. Percy was a girl. Percy was blind.

X

TOPSY-TURVY

"Back to back," said Percy. "I want to know which of you is which and who is taller than who."

She felt our heads and patted our hair.

"Right, which is the short one?"

"Me," I said, "Roly."

"What colour are your eyes?" she asked.

"Blue – and I've got freckles, like you."

Percy ran her fingers lightly over Judd's head and face. "Springy hair," she said. "Is it carrotty?"

"Yup," said Judd, "but no freckles."

"Your nose turns upwards," smiled Percy. "What colour are *your* eyes?"

"Brown."

"Like mine," said Percy.

"Why *are* you called Percy?" asked Judd. "It's a funny name for a girl, really."

"Yes," I said. "We thought you were going to be a weedy *boy*!"

Percy and Mr. Green laughed.

65

"Why should Percy be weedy?" protested Mr. Green.

I thought about it. "I really don't know. I've got very strong ideas about names."

"So I gathered from your homework," said Mr. Green.

"I'm not Percy at all, really," said Percy. "I'm Persephone."

"What?" spluttered Judd.

"PER-SEPH-ON-*Y*," said Percy.

We said nothing.

"Well," said Percy. 'Now you know why I don't use it every day. The first Persephone was not an everyday sort of person. Half the year she walked across the earth, and when she did the spring came and the summer too, but the other half she had to spend underneath the ground in the cold and the dark, and when she was down there it was autumn and winter up here. Well, I stay here all the time – just Percy, Percy Green. Dad, I'd like to take Judd and Roly for a walk and show them round."

I definitely remembered Aunt Lundy saying Mr. Green needed help. Percy seemed so happy and strong. What on earth could we do for her? I fingered my compass as we set off. Perhaps she wouldn't quite know which way to go.

"Come on Barney," said Percy, slipping a sturdy lead onto his collar. "You need showing round too."

"Have you always been blind?" asked Judd, striding along beside Percy.

"No," said Percy. "It happened when I was about nine. So I can remember things quite well, especially colours, and if you name things I can mostly see what they're like inside my head and of course my finger-tips help me a lot. If we go somewhere new my parents describe everything and I touch things as much as I can and get the feel of them, or the smell of them, or the sound of them."

We were walking down a chalky lane with a low hedgerow.

"What flowers are out now?" asked Percy.

We looked around.

"We-ell, there's a lot of that white stuff with long, thickish stalks – flat flowers with a lot of pollen, so the bees can sit on them," I said.

"Let's see," she said. We guided her just a little towards the flowers and she patted their tops and smelled them. "Oh, that's cow parsley – or is it Queen Anne's lace? I never know which is which."

"There are poppies, too," said Judd. "Shall I pick one for you?"

"No," said Percy, "they always droop and die. Let me just feel them – they're so silky and red, like blood." She stroked the petals and her fingertips were smudged with pollen. She lifted her head and sniffed the air. "We must be nearly at the bend where you'll catch sight of the sea. There's a stile there, and if we climb over and cut across the field you can take a quick look. Let's save the beach till later – I think Dad has a plan for tonight."

"Do you remember butterflies?" asked Judd.

"Dimly," said Percy, "but perhaps I imagine them even more beautiful than they are. Do you think they feel like those poppy petals?"

"I don't know," admitted Judd. "I've never touched one." He bent down.

"Here you are, Percy," he said, gruffly. "Here's a nice stone you can hold in your hand." He pressed into her palm a large round pebble. Her fingers closed over it and she smiled.

"Thanks."

"Here's the stile," I said. We clambered over, helping Percy in our clumsy way. We were in a cliffy field, very near the sea, with a salty wind blowing straight off it. Judd and I couldn't resist edging close to the steep edge that sloped down to the beach. Percy stood back, holding Barney's lead; she seemed to know exactly where we were.

"Be careful," she said. "It's steeper than you think."

"What's that funny little house out on those rocks?" I asked, peering down.

"That's St. George's Chapel-at-the-End," said Percy.

"At the end of what?" asked Judd.

"The end of land, end of sea – depends which way you're looking. Come on. Time to go home, now you know the lie of the land. There's a short cut across this field to the farm."

We skirted a blowy barley field, slipped down into

a copse of silvery green trees and came quite soon to the farm. We stopped and leaned on the gate into the yard. I felt lazy, friendly, free.

It was well past lunchtime.

"It's very quiet," said Judd.

"It's still early for milking," replied Percy. "They've probably all gone to cut the first barley."

"Shall we go and find something to eat?" I asked.

Suddenly Barney started whimpering, though I couldn't see why.

Percy turned round and bent over the dog.

"I can hear it too, boy," she whispered. "It's coming from over there."

Barney was straining on his lead.

"Open the gate quickly," said Percy. "Something's wrong – over there – " She was pointing to a shed across the yard. We opened the gate and hurried through.

Then I heard it too. A strange noise – hoarse breathing, hooves slithering, a horrid choking noise.

"I don't like the sound of that at all," said Percy. "Hurry, boys, hurry! Barney! Go for Dad! Go on! Dad! Fetch him! Fetch him! Good boy!"

Barney hesitated, ears pricked, eyes bright, tongue panting, and then he was off. Judd and I had run on ahead and rushed into the shed. It took a minute for our eyes to get used to the darkness.

"Look!" cried Judd. "Over there! It's a calf! It's halter's too tight. It's strangling itself."

Percy came up behind us.

"We must do something quickly," she cried. "There's no one else nearby."

"Your knife, Judd!" I cried.

The halter was made of thick rope, tied through a ring on the wall. Now it was tight round the calf's neck. It's eyes were bulging with terror. The more it pulled and twisted, the tighter the rope grew. Percy quietly slipped close to the calf, stroking it and talking softly. Judd fumbled for his knife.

"It'll be too blunt," he muttered. "I can't cut through *that*."

"If it's sharp enough to skin rabbits . . ." I said.

"I was boasting a bit."

"Just try," said Percy.

Where the rope was taut between the wall and the calf's trembling neck Judd began to hack and saw. At first very little happened. The calf grew more and more frantic, kicking out and gasping horribly.

Suddenly the rope began to fray, first one outer strand, then another and another till all at once it gave way completely.

The calf was still very frightened. It trembled from head to foot, its beautiful big brown eyes rolling wildly. Percy kept her hand on its restless flank and slowly I moved nearer.

Judd just stood staring, first at his knife, then at the calf and back at his knife again.

"Better shut the door. She might try to get out," I said.

"Here come Dad and Barney."

Sure enough I heard someone running and then, with Barney at his heels, Mr. Green came in a rush through the doorway. He took in the whole picture very quickly, Percy gently patting the nervous calf, the frayed fallen rope and Judd gingerly running his thumb along the knife edge.

"Barney, sit!" said Mr. Green. His voice was firm but very soft. "Everybody quiet. Roly, fetch some of that hay and then everybody go outside. We'll close the bottom of the stable door, and you boys can run and tell Mr. Stubbs."

"Well, Percy! I didn't promise you *heroes*!" Mr. Green laughed; Percy smiled. Judd looked as if he was going to cry, and I felt thoroughly warm inside.

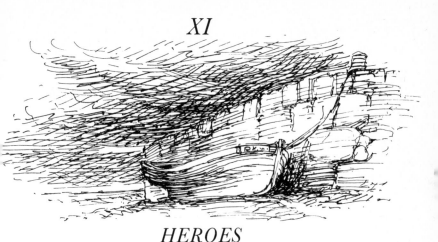

XI

HEROES

"Anybody got the strength left for a barbecue supper on the beach?" asked Mr. Green. "That was to be the highlight of your short visit, but after your brave deeds this afternoon it may seem rather an anti-climax. What do you say?"

"I say great," said Judd.

We were all stretched out on the grass by the barn in the sun. There are afternoons in summer that you feel will last forever.

"I say great too."

"It's more like a holiday every minute," said Judd.

"Enjoy what comes," said Percy and Mr. Green in one breath. They laughed. They were really happy. I had a sudden thought: punishment or holiday? Why did it have to be one or the other? It was it.

Then Judd said, "Well, whatever it is, I'm just glad I'm here."

"Me too."

73

"What's the menu, Dad?" said Percy.

"Check it through, Percy. Have I put in everything we need?"

Mr. Green put a large basket down beside Percy. Her fingers knew exactly the shape and feel of everything. "Sausages, bread, matches, butter, squashy tomatoes – oh Dad!" Percy groaned. "How often have I told you to put them at the top? Melon is it? Melon for a treat, and," she paused, "a bottle of cider, I hope!"

"Cider it is," said Mr. Green.

"You said *mackerel*," Judd moaned. "You said *fishing*."

"Yes, I did," said Mr. Green. "What I *didn't* say was, please go for a very long walk and then just for extras rescue a strangling calf."

"If we all collect the wood," said Percy, "we can fit in a row before we come home, even put a line out for mackerel – just in case."

Judd beamed at Percy.

"In you all get then," cried Mr. Green, moving towards the car.

We helped Percy into the front with the heavy basket, and scrambled into the back with Barney, who thumped his tail and licked our faces.

"Here we go," cried Mr. Green. "Firewood, fry, Flotsam and fish," and he put his foot down and whizzed us off to the beach, screeching just a little on the corners.

"What's Flotsam?" asked Judd.

"A very old rowing-boat," said Mr. Green. "Scruffy but seaworthy."

He pulled up at the edge of the beach and pointed.

"There she is, moored to the sea wall. We'll take her out after supper, but first let's all collect the wood and get the fire started."

Now came the strangest hours yet that day. Everything changed for us after that evening.

Holding Barney's lead, Percy moved easily along the beach. She heard the incoming tide before we saw it. She was the first to take her shoes off and scuff her feet happily through the sand. We wandered beside her picking up armfuls of driftwood and dried, crackling, popping seaweed until our noses were almost resting on our loads.

"That's enough," laughed Mr. Green who was pretty bowed down himself.

"We must be just below the chapel now," said Percy. "Shall we make the fire here, in the shelter of the rock?"

"Good idea," said Mr. Green.

We put down our wood and I turned to the sea. Suddenly I could not bear it that Percy was blind, and in the same moment I felt how lucky I was to be able to see and move as and how I wished. And I couldn't bear feeling how lucky I was, either. I began to run before I knew it down towards the water. I heard someone running after me. It was Judd. Then I stumbled in my bare feet over something lumpy, soggy and sticky.

"Ugh!" cried Judd. "How revolting." We were tripping over dead seagulls, scattered just above the water line, but they weren't just dead from old age or whatever usually makes seagulls die. You could see they were dead from oil. They were drenched black in it, sludgily choked inside and out. I felt sick.

"Here's another one, and another one," he sobbed.

"Well at least Percy can't see *that*."

We stared at the birds; the warm little waves, fresh and cheeky played over our toes. The sun's last rays sank into our backs. The wet sand felt good between our toes. The air blew soft and alive around us and into us. I looked out to the horizon – such a weird silver line that never goes away.

Judd looked up from the birds, and back to Percy. She was sitting cross-legged on the sand, her chin resting in her hand. She looked sad and lonely.

"Poor Percy," he said. "I wonder what she's thinking about."

"Is this the punishment then, do you think?" I asked Judd.

"You mean all this?" said Judd waving his arm to make a circle of sky, sea, and the Greens, the dead birds and us.

"Yes, I suppose so."

"Do you mean having a great time and feeling helpless about Percy and admiring her and sorry for her and lucky not to be blind and . . ."

"Yes."

"Well, it's not at all what I'd call punishment, like being hit or sent to your room, or no pocket money," said Judd.

"It's worse. It's all mixed up. It makes me feel funny."

"Like you don't quite know any more what's what," agreed Judd.

"What can we do for her?" I asked.

"I don't know, Roly. She seems quite able to look after herself."

"There must be something she wants."

"Well, let's ask her."

"No," I said. "Well – not just like that. Let's see if we can find out without actually asking."

"She might say something," said Judd, "which would give us an idea."

"Come on, you two!" called Mr. Green. "Fire's lit and Percy wants to show you something while the bangers are frying."

We ran back up the beach, determined to be on guard for any clues to Percy's greatest wish.

"Come and see St. George-at-the-End," said Percy.

"Oh!" we both mumbled. What a disappointment, going to see an old church.

"Yes, sure, Percy," said Judd brightly, giving me a funny look.

"Can you steer me up on to the path?" asked Percy. "Barney's fallen asleep."

"Sure! 'Course we can." We both spoke at once.

77

"The path's very narrow – why don't I go in front, and Roly at the back? Put your hand on my shoulder, Percy," said Judd, very much the boss all of a sudden. "And if Roly puts his hand on your shoulder we'll keep together nicely."

We set off up the short path.

I did hope Percy wasn't suddenly going to be all holy. I really wasn't interested in churches.

Judd stopped at the little grey stone porch in front of a heavy wooden door.

"How do you know it isn't locked up?" he asked in a hopeful sort of voice.

"Hope the bangers don't burn," said I out loud, by mistake really.

Percy laughed.

"Don't worry," she said. "We're not going in, but here, come and see this wall."

She was groping in a dark corner.

"Ah!" she said happily. "Here it is!"

From Percy's face you would have thought she was looking at her favourite picture and that's exactly what she was doing.

Judd and I peered over her shoulder.

Percy's fingers were moving over a picture carved deep in the stone.

"What's it of?" said Judd. "I can hardly see."

"Is that a dragon?" I asked.

"Yes, and here, tied to a tree, is a princess."

"And who's that on a charging horse with a great long sword?" said Judd. "Oh, gosh, I know," he added quickly. "It's St. George, of course. St. George and the dragon and all that!"

He looked pleased with himself. "That's my real name, you know, George."

"I know," said Percy. "Dad told me how you think it's cooler to call yourself Judd."

"Well, I never thought about George being a brave man's name."

"He's your hero," said Percy. "He killed the fiery dragon who got between him and the princess." She ran her fingers again over the figures. "I bet he was terrified of the dragon. It's much bigger and more powerful than him. He must have wanted to reach the princess very much."

I stared and stared at the dragon. There was something odd about it.

"Do you know, Percy," I said. "That dragon looks as if it actually wants to be killed. It's begging for something. You can see it in it's eyes."

I could have bitten my tongue off when I'd said that.

"Can you? Can you really?" said Percy excitedly. "That makes sense. It must be lonely being a dragon, puffing and raging with fire, everybody hating you and being afraid of you. Perhaps this dragon was ready for a change."

Judd was almost smirking by now. You'd have thought he was St. George himself.

"What about me?" said I.

"Oh, Roly!" cried Percy. "Don't you know about

Roland and his horn? He saved a king's life! He was such a great hero, he had his own song!"

"But he wasn't called Smith," I said glumly.

"Why do you think there are so many Smiths?" demanded Percy.

"I don't know," I shrugged.

"Because they've always been needed!" said Percy. "Think how many horses still need shoeing. Only smiths know how to heat and bend metal for a thousand things. Smiths are very, very important."

"All that," I mumbled, "makes my song sound really stupid."

"Well, you can change it," said Percy.

"That would be wrong, because I felt like what I wrote when I wrote it. But I could add some bits on, couldn't I?"

"Of course!" said Percy. "Come on, we must get back down and help Dad. Lead on Judd – or George!"

"I've got a saint and Roly's got a song," said Judd. "What about you Percy?" He nudged me hard. "Would you have liked to be a princess and be rescued from a dragon?"

"Not really," grinned Percy. "But," she paused, "but I would like to have ridden a bike." There was gritty hurt in her voice.

I was stunned, and Judd's mouth fell open. Percy shook herself, as if to break her dream. "Gosh, I'm hungry, aren't you?"

Ride a bike! Percy ride a bike? What a thought!

Close to the friendly rosy fire, as we munched our sausages and sizzling fried bread slithering with sloshy tomatoes, Judd and I chewed on the thought.

The moon came up. The world turned silver and we went off for a row in Flotsam. As I watched Percy take an oar and give Judd his first rowing lesson, as I watched Mr. Green put out a mackerel line, I wondered and wondered how on earth Percy could ever ride a bike.

"Good heavens!" cried Mr. Green suddenly. "We have actually caught a fish!"

He pulled the line in and sure enough there lay one good-sized glittering mackerel. Judd looked at me and smiled.

He smiled and smiled.

"Great day, eh, Roly?" he said "Great night: barbecue, beach, rowing, fishing and all that, eh?"

"Yes." I smiled back, but sighed inside.

Over the voice of Percy talking to her Dad as he

unhooked the fish and she turned the boat to shore, Judd whispered to me:

"*Tandem,* Roly. *Tandem!*"

The song goes on
I have new friends
But a dog is dead
Now Percy's turned things upside down
Light, dark, sad, bright
Could I be a hero?
Ordinary plus?
I don't know
But the song goes on . . .

XII

MR. TYLER'S
TURN

"He *what?*" gasped Mr. Tyler.

"He saved its life," said I.

"You're trying to tell me my son, my son George, saved that calf's life?" said Mr. Tyler.

"That's right, he saved it's life."

Mr. Tyler stared a long time at Judd.

"I'll never understand you kids," he sighed. "One day you run off with a valuable dog which, thanks to you, gets run over; then you come and tell me you've saved a life! Well I'm blowed, George. I hardly knew you had it in you."

"It wasn't just me," said Judd. "Roly and Percy were there too, Dad."

"Percy!" Mr. Tyler laughed. "You and your Percy. It's been nothing but 'Percy this' and 'Percy that' ever since you got in that door. Funny name for a girl, I must say."

We had gone straight to Judd's place when Mr. Green and Percy dropped us back in town the very next day on their way to join Mrs. Green. Only Mr. Tyler was at home when we came charging in. At first he was quite gruff and frosty. You could tell he wasn't really listening to us. He stood in the kitchen doorway slapping his newspaper into the palm of his hand. We both tumbled round him and poured out our story in a right old jumble. But what got to him, of course, was Percy.

"Percy a girl?" he interrupted. "Blind?"

He sat down.

"Poor kid," he said, still gruff, with his head down, punching at the cushion a bit.

"Well," he said, still gruff, but not so frosty, "so – you had a good time. There's this blind girl you feel really sorry for. And now you want to do something for her. Is that it? Have I got it right?"

"Yes, Dad," said Judd. "That's it exactly. She wants to ride a bike – "

"Ride a bike?" laughed Mr. Tyler. "Don't be daft. How could she possibly ride a *bike*?"

"No-no," I rushed in. "Of course she couldn't, but she could ride a tandem. It was George who thought of that," I added.

"Was it now?" said Mr. Tyler. "And what did *you* get from this outing, Roly Smith?" he asked. "George saved a calf. George is full of good ideas. So what about *you*, eh, Roly Smith? What about *you*?"

How could I tell him what I had felt on the beach –
about the togetherness of things – not just the eithers
and the ors? I couldn't tell Mr. Tyler that, but there
was something I could say.

"Well, Percy showed me I didn't have much to
moan about."

"Stopped feeling sorry for yourself, eh?" said Mr.
Tyler.

"Don't suppose it'll last, but yes. Yes," I repeated.
"Definitely." I paused. "Mr. Tyler, how can we get
hold of a tandem? Do you know how much they
cost?"

"A new tandem?" Mr. Tyler whistled. "Phew, you
must be joking. Why, a new bike can cost you well
over a hundred quid, so we could be talking about
three or four hundred pounds!"

Judd and I stared at him. Of course we knew it was
probably true. We just hadn't thought it through.

"We could never save that up in five days," sighed
Judd.

"Five days," laughed Mr. Tyler. "Not even five
months; five years, more like."

And then his face changed. I could tell he was
suddenly really thinking about Percy being blind and
wanting to ride a bike.

"Why did you say five days?" he asked.

"Well, that's all the time we've got. The Greens
are coming home then and we had this idea if we
could get Percy a tandem as a surprise, see – "

"She wants it so much," Judd interrupted. "You could tell by her voice. We want her to have it *now*, to show her – just to show her we care."

"We want her to have some ordinary fun," I said.

"Like us," added Judd.

"All right, all right. Now shut up the two of you, and sit down. How can a man think with all this nattering and fidgeting?"

We did as we were told. The room was now so quiet you could have heard a fly sneeze.

The silence went on for a long, long time. Then Mr. Tyler put his hand in his pocket and fished out a grubby little diary.

"'Course I'll have to put it on the grapevine PDQ," he said to himself.

"Grapevine?" asked Judd.

"PDQ?" I muttered.

Mr. Tyler sighed and raised his eyes to some invisible friend on the ceiling.

"Spread the word," he explained, "pretty damn quick. If you want a tandem ready for your friend Percy by Saturday, you can thank your lucky stars I have my contacts. I believe I know every scrap merchant for miles around."

"Dad!" gasped Judd, jumping to his feet. "Do you mean you're going to help us? That's great! I mean, you're great, you're really great!"

Mr. Tyler tried not to look pleased.

"You'd better start believing in miracles," he said sharply. "Tandems don't grow on trees. Now, clear out, the two of you. I've got a lot of 'phone calls to make. George, nip down to the shop and give your mother a hand."

"Thanks, Mr. Tyler," I said. "I'll be off home now."

"Is your aunt in on this already, Roly?" he called after me.

"No, Mr. Tyler, we came straight here."

"Oh, you did, did you?" Mr. Tyler sounded pleased.

He'd roared at us
He'd raged at us
He'd even wanted us hit
But now here comes a miracle –
He has his other side.

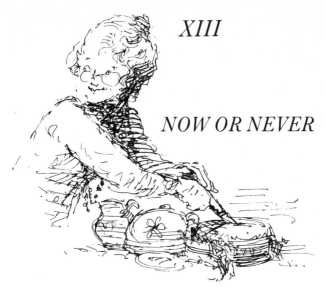

XIII

NOW OR NEVER

When I came bounding home Aunt Lundy gave me a clumsy hug, and then a slice of cake. It was not her way to bother with "Hullo," "How are you?" or "Had a nice time?"

"Thanks, Aunt Lundy," I said, through a mouthful. "Can you believe it – Mr. Tyler is actually, at this *very* moment, spreading the word – on his grapevine – spreading the word – he says he knows all the scrap dealers for miles around – and he'll have them all looking for a tandem!"

"A tandem?" Aunt Lundy prodded at her hairpins looking puzzled. Then she smiled. "Oh, for Percy, d'you mean? What a wonderful idea, Roly! Did you think of that?"

"No. It was Judd. But – but –" I spluttered, cake crumbs flying all over the place, "how did *you* know?"

"I didn't – well, not about the tandem . . ."

"But you knew about Percy all the time, didn't you? Before we went off?"

"Mm, I did," she admitted. "Mr. Green told me about her on Sunday, when I went to the pub with him."

"Aunt Lundy, you really are a crafty . . ."

"Old nosy-parker, eh?" She pushed at her wispy hair and blushed, just a bit. She looked quite apologetic. "I thought it would be better all round if you met Percy – fresh, so to speak."

"Yes. Yes, I see."

"But tell me now about the tandem," urged Aunt Lundy.

"Mr. Tyler's really keen to help us get one for Percy. We want to do it now, have it ready when the Greens come back on Saturday. Mr. Tyler told us to start believing in miracles. Do you think we've got a chance, Aunt Lundy? Oh say yes, say yes."

"But today's Tuesday!" cried Aunt Lundy. "Goodness, that *is* cutting it fine."

Said out loud it sounded absolutely crazy. I knew Judd would feel the same. It just would not be the same if we found a tandem in everybody's own good time. I sat down on the stairs and put my head in my hands.

"Miracles do happen, you know, Roly," said Aunt Lundy. "We must hang on a bit and give Mr. Tyler and his friends time. It's Mr. Tyler's show after all and he is a business man; if he knows all the scrap-dealers for miles around there must be a good chance a tandem will turn up. More cake?"

"No thanks."

"Why don't you go and say, 'Hullo,' to Everest?" asked Aunt Lundy, disappearing into the kitchen.

True to his name, Everest was, as usual, asleep.

That was Tuesday afternoon.

Wednesday passed without a sound. The 'phone didn't ring once. Aunt Lundy became very strict; kept me busy and said I must leave the Tylers in peace for at least one more day; it was rude to harass Mr. Tyler and might make him wish he'd never offered to help.

On Thursday morning Aunt Lundy went to the shops and I rang Judd up every half an hour.

"Dad's getting fed up with you," said Judd after my fourth call. "He says you'd better come over here. That way at least our line won't be engaged all the time. Oh do come over, Roly," Judd begged. "I've got to clean out all the hutches and cages. It's no fun all by myself, but at least it's something to do and you can hear the 'phone from the back of the shop."

"I'll be right there," I said and turned round to find Aunt Lundy coming in the door.

"No word, eh?" she said. "Time *is* running out. It would have been such fun, and more than fun, to have got up this marvellous surprise in time for Saturday. But you know, Roly, it just may not work. It may take much longer."

My face fell a mile.

"But – but – we've got to," I cried. "It just won't be the same if – *one* day – perhaps halfway through next year – someone comes up with a tandem."

"I know the feeling," agreed Aunt Lundy. "Now or never. Now or never," she said again. "That's it! You're going round to the Tylers? Right! I'm coming with you. I think we can both be helpful at this point."

And she hurried me off to the pet shop, muttering to herself all the way.

"Poor Mr. Tyler. Bitten off more than he can chew . . . Poor Percy. . . Two heads are sometimes better than one. . . Don't want to chivvy all the same. Not much time left. Might not like me interfering, but in a way, for my sins, I started all this."

And so on and so on all the way to the Tylers.

XIV

GOINGS AND COMINGS

When we got to the shop Mr. Tyler was just putting the phone down and Mrs. Tyler was in a fluster, trying to serve three customers at once.

"Glad you brought your aunt with you, Roly," said Mr. Tyler. "Come through quick. We've not much time. I've news at last. George! Where's George got to?"

Aunt Lundy smiled at me as we followed Mr. Tyler into the back of the shop.

"Quick march! Quick march!" screeched an unexpected voice.

"Shut up, Parker," said Judd, scrambling to his feet from among the rabbit hutches.

Parker the parrot, of course. I had forgotten the fright he'd given me the first time I came to the pet shop.

"What's up, Dad?" Judd asked eagerly.

"That was my old mate, Charlie, fifty miles up the motorway. Says he was just driving off out of an old

93

car dump he uses with a full load on when he spotted a tandem lying in the corner in a nettlebed."

"Oh great!" cried Judd.

"He says it looked to be in poor condition," went on Mr. Tyler. "Poor condition, mind; says no way could he have piled one more thing onto his lorry and hasn't got time to go back." Mr. Tyler turned to Aunt Lundy. "Thing is, I'm almost as dead set on this tandem idea as these boys, but I don't like to leave the shop. . . ."

"Harry," sang out Mrs. Tyler, "we're getting low on birdseed and we need more hay bags bringing in."

"See what I mean," said Mr. Tyler.

I churned inside with excitement and impatience.

Why do grown-ups take so long to decide things? Suddenly I heard my own voice, loud, clear and rather bossy. "Coming, Mrs. Tyler. Aunt Lundy and I can help here, can't we, Aunt Lundy?"

"But of course we can," said Aunt Lundy. "Why doesn't Judd go with you?" she said to Mr. Tyler. "It'll take two of you to load it up."

Hurry, hurry, I was saying to myself behind my teeth. There's no time to lose. Someone might get there before us. I was almost jumping up and down on my toes.

Judd came to the rescue.

"Yes, that's a great idea. Come on Dad! Let's go *now*."

"The boys are right, Mr. Tyler," said Aunt Lundy quickly. "Off you go and don't worry about a thing.

Roly will fetch hay and whatever else is needed and I'll help Mrs. Tyler. I've always wanted to work in a shop."

"Bettah late than nevah," bawled the parrot.

"Shut up, Parker," Judd said.

And then we were all moving as if we were in a speeded up film. Aunt Lundy rushed off to the shop. I ran for hay bags. Mr. Tyler grabbed his keys and Judd was out of the door and into the car before you could say knife.

"Roly!" called Mrs. Tyler. "You'd best pick up where George left off. Finish cleaning those hutches. Then you can feed the pups and the kittens."

"Don't muck about!" screeched Parker.

Aunt Lundy trotted about weighing birdseed into little brown bags as if she'd been doing it all her life; by lunch-time she'd made her first sale – a goldfish.

"You see," I heard her say to Mrs. Tyler, "business as usual!"

"Well, I must say," said Mrs. Tyler, "you've taken to it like a duck to water."

I heard them prattling away to each other and the customers all afternoon.

Meanwhile I began to feel a bit sorry for myself. Every time I stopped for a second to play with a pup or dangle a carrot under a rabbit's twitching nose that wretched Parker would screech, "Don't muck about! Don't muck about!" It began to sound more and more like Mr. Tyler in a bad mood.

Just before the shop shut Aunt Lundy sold three

songbirds. That really made her day, and Mrs. Tyler was so pleased she went off to buy some buns.

I sat down on a hay bale and let myself get mopey. I was tired and very sweaty and dirty. Aunt Lundy and Judd were having all the fun. I felt as if I'd been pushed out of my own adventure. What was keeping Judd and Mr. Tyler anyway? It was nearly six o'clock. They'd left before lunch. Perhaps someone else had found the tandem before they got there. Perhaps they were trailing up the motorway, further and further away, seeking out other dumps and it was all a wild goose chase.

Suddenly I heard a car coming, then brakes being slammed on. The beastly Parker flapped his wings.

"Bettah late than nevah!" he squawked.

Judd came rushing in.

"We've done it," he cried. "We've got it! Come and see, come and see!"

"Quick march! Quick march!" screamed Parker.

"Oh shut up Parker," said Judd.

"What took you so long?" I asked, hurrying after him. "You've been ages."

"First we got lost, then we had a puncture on our way out of the dump. There was broken glass everywhere, and then we went to see the Greens."

"You *what?*" I yelled.

"Oh, never mind now," said Judd. He looked grubby and tired too. "Just look at it."

And look I did.

My heart bumped with shock.

Propped against the car was a tandem all right; but talk about rusty, dusty, battered and bent.

"It needs a lot of work," said Mr. Tyler, wiping his hands on a hanky. "A lot of work."

"We've got a deadline, see," said Judd. "The Greens are coming here at five o'clock on Saturday afternoon."

"On Saturday afternoon?" I echoed. "Hey – what was that you said about going to *see* them? They weren't there, were they?"

"Came home early," said Mr. Tyler. "Bad weather."

"So Mrs. Green couldn't get on with her painting," said Judd. "And no fun for Percy, just driving about in the car . . . "

"But what made you think of going there anyway?"

"Well," said Judd, "I said to Dad, how're we going to get them here? They haven't got a telephone at the barn. So we thought we'd just drop by and leave a note, but when we get there we see their car, so . . . ."

"Gosh!" I cried, "I hope you didn't give the game away."

"Don't worry," said Mr. Tyler. "We only saw Mr. Green: the other two were down on the beach."

"George here says we were just passing," added Mr. Tyler. "Says we wanted to leave an invitation for them to come and see the animals and have tea by way of thanking them for all they'd done for you, see?

97

'How about Saturday?' says George and, 'Saturday it is,' says Mr. Green."

"Don't worry, Roly," said Judd. "Dad'll get the bent bits straight. He's got brawny arms. We'll get it done in time."

"If we all lend a hand," said Aunt Lundy from the doorway.

"We'll need something for all that rust," I said.

"And a puncture outfit," added Judd.

"Big can of paint," muttered Mr. Tyler.

"And some polish for the chrome," said Mrs. Tyler, joining Aunt Lundy in the doorway.

"But first, fish and chips all round, I'd say," put in Mr. Tyler.

"Then an early night," said Mrs. Tyler and Aunt Lundy in a chorus.

"Quick march! Quick march!" screamed Parker.

"Shut up, Parker," said Judd and I together and laughed and grinned and yawned and stopped worrying.

XV

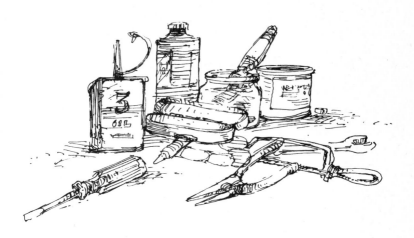

HARD WORK IN A HURRY

"Puncture outfit, my eye," said Mr. Tyler next day as he watched us pumping and pumping away. "The treads are all right mind, but you need new tubes. Better run down to Bell's Bikes straightaway and pick up a pair."

"How much do you think they'll be?"

Mr. Tyler looked at me crossly.

"Never mind about that," he barked. "Mr. Bell's expecting you in today for a few bits and pieces. I saw him in the pub last night. Told him the story. . ."

"That's kind of him," I said.

"Kind of him?" echoed Judd. "Why, it's amazing,

amazing, that's what! He never usually buys even one raffle ticket off me *and* he's got three kids at our school."

"That's enough of that," said Mr. Tyler. "Don't think you're the only ones who'd like to do a good turn to a blind kid. You just get on down there now while I get these spokes straightened out."

"Grown-ups can be right soft," said Judd when we were out in the street.

"I'm glad they can be. Come on. Race you to Bell's Bikes."

Not only did Mr. Bell give us the inner tubes, but oil as well and some really good stuff for stopping rust. We tried to thank him but he wouldn't have it.

"You'd better get a move on, or your paint won't be dry in time!"

"Paint!" panted Judd as we hurried off. "I forgot about paint."

"We've got to get all that rust off first before we can *think* about paint." I said, pushing open the door and nearly falling over Aunt Lundy.

"Whoops!" she cried. "Paint, did you say? Here's paint. I chose red. Felt somehow it was a colour that would get through to Percy."

She held the can out to us.

"Gosh, thanks, Aunt Lundy. Everyone's being so kind."

"Don't thank me. I just popped into that Do-It-Yourself place and got talking to such a nice young man. When I mentioned what you boys were doing he flatly refused to let me pay. Said to tell you to be sure to paint the bike in a really good light as it was rather a fiddly job . . . Oh yes! And to use the right-sized brush – not too large – and . . . Oh yes! This paint dries extra fast. I must go . . . It's time for my turn in the shop."

Off she went and in came Mrs. Tyler.

"Here you are, boys. Rags, wire brush and wire wool. It's like Brillo, see." She pulled off a piece of wire wool and attacked the rusty metal work. "Rub it down really well – get all the knobbly bits off before you put that anti-rust stuff on and be sure to let that dry off before you start painting. I'll bring you some tea in a minute."

And she hurried away.

"Grown-ups can be right bossy," said Judd. "They all want to be in on the act."

We picked up the wire wool and began to rub and rub, then to brush the spokes really well.

"Still," I said, sneezing as the rusty dust began to fly and the wire wool tickled my nose, "still, if you think what things were like a week ago, with everyone furious with us and arguing about us, I'd rather have it like this."

Judd stopped work for a minute.

"Do you – do you – think about him much?" he asked.

I went on rubbing and brushing. I didn't want to look at Judd.

"D'you mean, about Hannibal?"

"Yes," said Judd. "Do you?"

I stopped and looked at him.

"Yes, though I can hardly bear it. I'll never forget what happened, as long as I live. Will you?"

"No," he said. "I go all cold when I think about that pup, because I can't ever undo what I did."

"*We* did," I said.

"Well, *I* started it."

"But if we hadn't gone off with Hannibal, none of this would have happened."

"Who'd have thought it," said Judd. "Us two, trying to get a tatty old bike together for a girl."

"Not *any* girl, though," I said.

"You'll have to work quicker than that," interrupted Mrs. Tyler, coming in again with two mugs of tea. "Here, let me have a go. I said it's like Brillo."

"Thanks, Mum, but we're doing all right."

"Have it your own way. But give me a shout when it comes to polishing the chrome. I love a shine, a really nice shine."

"All right, Mum," grinned Judd. "Don't get carried away."

"I know when I'm not wanted!" Mrs. Tyler laughed, bustling away.

"Come on," said Judd. "We'd better get the tubes in and then we can start painting."

All day long the grown-ups popped in and out: Mr. Tyler to test the brakes, Aunt Lundy to peer at the chain and remind us to give it plenty of oil; Mr. Tyler again, to point out that we'd left rust on the pedals;

Mrs. Tyler with pasties and more tea, telling us to clean up as we went along.

It was helpful in an annoying sort of way.

By five o'clock we were ready to paint. It was a race against time in the summer evening light. The atmosphere was tense. The grown-ups faded away. No more talk, no more tea. Just the two of us; just paint, paint, paint with fine brushes, trying not to get in each other's way, trying not to make splodges or crooked lines . . . till – all of a sudden – it was over. It was done.

We stood over the tandem, dusty, oily, smelling of paint and turpentine.

"Can't wait to see her face," said Judd. "Can't wait to see her face!"

Hard work in a hurry?
Never mind
Oily and dirty?
Never mind
Grown-ups bossy?
Grown-ups kind?
That's all right
The sun is just about to set
And Percy's tandem's ready . . .

XVI

END OR BEGINNING?

I slept over at Judd's place that night and straight after breakfast we rushed back to the bike.

There it stood, gleaming and brave, waiting now for Percy.

"Is the paint dry?" said Judd.

Nervously I prodded at it with a fingertip. "Still just a little bit tacky. Better leave it alone for a bit."

There was nothing to do now, except wait till tea-time. I know there are always sixty seconds to a minute, but some minutes seem like hours.

"What are we going to *do*?" moaned Judd. "It's ages till they come."

"Business as usual, as your aunt would say, Roly," boomed Mr. Tyler coming up behind us. "Saturday job, Saturday chores, George."

"Oh–oh," groaned Judd.

"Roly can help you," said Mr. Tyler.

"Quick march! Quick march! Don't muck about!" screeched a bossy voice.

"Oh, shut up, Parker," yelled Judd and I together. We headed dolefully for the hay and carrots, and silently set to work among the snuffly, squeaky, nibbling animals.

Then a funny thing happened. I felt empty inside like a balloon, when all the air's come out.

The magical excitement of that topsy-turvy day with Percy seemed like a dream. Had Judd and I gone a bit mad? Rushing off like that to find her a bike and getting the grown-ups all worked up too? I peeped at the bike through the window.

Gleaming and brave, I'd said? Well, now it looked ordinary too. Just an old second-hand or tenth-hand bike; not *that* fantastic. Perhaps Percy wouldn't think it was fantastic either.

I didn't dare tell Judd what I was thinking or what I was seeing. I just put my head down and decided to clean every single rabbit hutch really well and change every single water bowl of every single animal; just that, because it was smelly and wet and under my nose and real enough.

"Hey, Roly," laughed Judd. "What's come over you?"

"Don't know," I muttered.

Judd went to the window to look at the bike. I held my breath. What did it look like to him?

"Come and have a look at her," said Judd. "Doesn't she look great, Roly?"

Slowly I came to the window, and then another funny thing happened. The bike was gleaming again and the paint didn't look bad at all, and the sun was shining and a shivery feeling came back in me.

Time was full again; time for hamburgers over the road; time for the paint to dry; time for Mrs. Tyler to give the chrome her promised lovely shine; time to get the white mice out and let them run up and down inside our sweaters; time even to shut up shop half an hour early.

"Never done *that* before," said Mr. Tyler, "but then how often do girls called Percy come to collect bright red tandems from Tyler's Pet Shop; how often, eh?"

We all gathered round the bike again for one last good look at it.

"'Course," said Mr. Tyler, "you may have to adjust the saddle. No way of telling if we've got that right till Percy gives it a try."

Till Percy gives it a try.

My shivery feeling grew stronger. Any minute now she'd be here.

"Oh heck!" cried Judd. "I hope she likes it!"

"The saddles!" cried Mrs. Tyler. "I forgot to polish the saddles!"

"It's too late now," I said. "There's a car turning into the yard."

"Come on Harry," said Mrs. Tyler. "What're you

107

waiting for?" The Tylers went outside to meet them.

Then everything went wrong. Well, not wrong, but just not as we'd planned.

"I feel shy," said Judd.

"Me, too, but when they walk round that corner they're going to walk smack into the tandem, so come on, Judd, come on!"

"Oh heck, they're supposed to see the pets first."

I sort of pushed us both out of the door.

"Here they come," smiled Percy turning towards us. Barney's ears were pricked up and he was wagging his tail. We brought our shyness with us. It was all quiet, as if nobody knew what to do or say next. And then Judd let out a great yelp and burst into fits of laughter as if he was being tickled.

"George!" cried Mrs. Tyler. "Whatever's come over you, really! Where are your manners?"

"It's the mouse, the mouse!" he spluttered. "I forgot all about the mouse. It's tickling my neck. Get it off me, Roly! Quick, get it off me."

He was doubled up laughing and jumping about all over the place. He looked so funny that everyone began to laugh too. I ran my hand round the back of his neck and my hand closed on the little white mouse.

"Got him!" I cried.

"Can I hold him?" said Percy.

I put the mouse into Percy's hands.

"Will it run up my sleeve?"

"Sure," said Judd, guiding the mouse into Percy's

cuff. The next thing Percy was doubled up in fits of laughter as the mouse scurried bumpily up the inside of her sweater and down again.

Shyness went.

"Come on in everybody," said Mr. Tyler.

The minute they got round the corner Mr. and Mrs. Green saw the tandem, of course. They stopped and stared. Percy stopped because they had stopped and we all stopped too.

A new silence fell.

Mrs. Tyler put her finger to her lips and Mr. Tyler made frantic signs to Mr. Green, pointing now at the tandem, now at Percy, now at us.

Suddenly the light dawned. Mr. Green gave us a great smile but Mrs. Green began to sniff. She sniffed and sniffed, scrabbling in her pocket for a handkerchief.

"What's the matter, Mum?" asked Percy. "Are you getting a cold?"

"No, darling! I mean yes, darling."

"It's come on very suddenly," said Percy.

"Don't worry, darling."

"Come along, Percy, Barney. This way,' said Mr. Green, trying to steer her clear of the bike.

"Something in the way?" asked Percy.

All the grown-ups were now looking at me and Judd.

"Over to you," said their eyes.

Then Parker's bossy croak came through the open doorway.

"Don't muck about," he said. "Don't muck about."

That did it. Bossy old Parker got us past all the words, all the plans, got us to move. I slipped over to hold the bike. Judd went to Percy.

"Yes," he said, "something in the way, Percy."

"But only because we want it to be," I added. "It's for you, you see – for your own."

"Give us your hand a minute, Percy," said Judd.

She did. He led her right up to the bike.

"This is for you, see. For your own," he said. "Put your hand out – now, down a bit. That's it – and walk along slowly."

Percy's hands played over the bike, up and down, from end to end.

Rain and sun together make the rainbow.

Percy's rainbow came from a not-believing what her hands were telling her, from about five sparkling teardrops and the most beautiful smile I had ever seen.

"I don't believe it!" she said chokily. "For me? It's bright, isn't it? Red, is it?"

"Yes," said Judd and I together, mightily proud, mightily pleased.

"Hop on."

"Your body never forgets how to ride a bike," said Judd.

"Hope you're right," laughed Percy, climbing on with a bit of help from Mr. Green. "Where are we going?"

"To my house, for tea. My aunt's been longing to meet you," I said.

"What about Judd?" asked Percy.

"I've got my bike here. Roly and I will take turns to ride tandem. Come on, let's go."

"See you at Aunt Lundy's." I waved to all the grown-ups.

"I'm not dreaming am I, Dad?" called Percy.

"You are not dreaming," replied Mr. Green.

"Let's roll," shouted Judd.

We didn't exactly roll at first. We wobbled, clumsy and heavy, but then, as we picked up speed, we seemed to fly down the street by the canal towards the leafier roads that led to my house.

"This is my best day ever," cried Percy.

"And mine," yelled Judd.

"And mine. Your turn, Judd."

We changed places and I stood for a moment and watched them ride away.

The road ahead lay open, empty, calling.

I suddenly remembered my father's photos of the great mountains with the golden gaps between the peaks leading on and on forever and ever. I thought again of that silver line at the sea and how you can never quite be sure where sky ends and sea begins.

I climbed onto Judd's bike and set off after the other two.

Was this an end or a beginning? I didn't know, but I was happy, Judd was happy and Percy was happy and I was sure there'd be two kinds of cake for tea.

> *I am twelve years old*
> *Size seven are my shoes*
> *And I am not growing upwards*
> *But I've grown into my name*
> *Judd is my friend*
> *Percy has her bike*
> *Let Everest sleep on*
> *And LONG LIVE EVERYTHING!*